STORMS AND THE EARTH

NIKKI BUNDEY

 Carolrhoda Books, Inc. / Minneapolis

First American edition published in 2001 by
Carolrhoda Books, Inc.

All the words that appear in **bold** type are explained
in the glossary that starts on page 30.

Carolrhoda Books, Inc.
A division of Lerner Publishing Group
241 First Avenue North
Minneapolis, MN 55401 U.S.A.

Website address: www.lernerbooks.com

A ZOË BOOK

Library of Congress Cataloging-in-Publication Data

Bundey, Nikki, 1948–
     Storms and the earth / by Nikki Bundey
          p. cm.—(The science of weather)
     Includes index.
     ISBN 1-57505-474-4 (lib. bdg. : alk. paper)
     1. Storms—Juvenile literature. 2. Weather—Juvenile literature.
     [1. Storms. 2. Weather.] I. Title. II. Series: Bundey, Nikki, 1948–
     The science of weather.
QC941.3.B86   2001
551.55—dc21   00-009386

Printed in Italy by Grafedit SpA
Bound in the United States of America
1 2 3 4 5 6—OS—06 05 04 03 02 01

CONTENTS

STORMY WEATHER

Lightning flashes, **thunder** crashes. Rain drums on the roof. Wind howls through the trees, and branches come tumbling down. Storms are exciting and sometimes a bit scary.

Storms bring extreme, violent weather conditions. Storms can be very dangerous, so don't go outside when it's stormy. It's best to stay safe in your home or school—but do watch what's going on from a window.

Storms affect the earth's surface in many different ways. High winds whip up waves at sea. These waves are hitting the coast of Brittany in France.

Storms can cause flooding. This is Mozambique in Africa. In 2000, Mozambique's rivers were already bursting their banks when one tropical storm after another hit the country. The rain fell in torrents for days on end.

Electrical storms are always dangerous. A sudden flash of lightning can kill you. Never take shelter beneath a tree during a storm, because the tree, and you, may be struck by lightning.

Storms can take different forms. The wind is usually very strong, and a storm might bring driving rain, snow, or sleet. Storm winds pick up dust and grit from the earth's surface. However, **electrical storms** often occur when the weather is still and hot. These storms bring thunder and lightning.

THE STORM FACTORY

Weather conditions on earth begin 93 million miles away in space. The sun's hot rays directly strike the central part of the earth, around the **equator**. In the extreme north and south, around the **poles**, the rays fall at a slant.

The equator gets very hot, while the poles are bitterly cold. Hot air rises, and cooler air rushes in to take its place. This rushing air makes winds that move across the planet.

The wind is rising. Why? The sun heats the **gases** in the air, or atmosphere, and makes them rise. Cooler air moves in below to take their place.

Big drops of rain begin to fall. Why? Heat from the sun turns water into an invisible gas called **water vapor**. As the vapor rises through the atmosphere, it cools and **condenses**. It turns back into **liquid** water and falls as rain.

The earth's "weather factory" can produce gentle, pleasant conditions. But it can also produce dangerous storms and foul weather.

The air, or **atmosphere**, presses down on the earth's surface. High **air pressure** brings sunny, clear weather. An area of low pressure brings cloudy or rainy weather.

Pressure systems whirl around as they move across the earth's surface. As one system gives way to another, high winds and storms might form.

GALE FORCE

We use the **Beaufort scale** to describe the strength of the winds. Winds at Force 8 are called fresh gales. They blow at speeds between 39 and 46 miles per hour. Twigs snap off trees. Force 9 (47–54 mph) winds are strong gales. Branches and shingles come crashing down into the street. Force 10 winds (55–63 mph) are called storms, and Force 11 winds (64–72 mph) are violent storms. They cause widespread damage.

Gales and storms at sea can tear the sails from a boat and break its mast. Huge waves can sink a ship or drive it onto rocks. This yacht has been blown onto rocks on the coast of Ireland.

Winds over Force 10 on the Beaufort scale are powerful enough to blow down trees. A storm has uprooted this big oak tree.

High winds rub objects with a force called **friction**. Winds pass easily over objects that are low lying or **streamlined**. Objects that stick out catch the wind's full force.

The greater the object's **wind resistance**, the more likely it is to be blown over. **Elastic** materials, such as the trunks of young trees, survive the wind's force by bending over. Stiffer, **brittle** materials, such as dead branches, snap easily.

See for Yourself
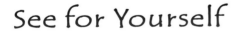

- On the morning after a big storm, go outside to look at the damage.
- Are there twigs or branches on the ground?
- Are whole trees uprooted?
- Are any tiles or shingles lying broken in the streets?
- Are any buildings damaged?
- Can you guess the force of the storm?

HURRICANE HAVOC

The strongest winds are rated as Force 12 (over 72 mph) on the Beaufort scale. These winds create fierce **tropical** storms. Tropical storms that start over the Atlantic Ocean are called **hurricanes**. Over the Indian Ocean, they are called **cyclones**. Over the Pacific Ocean, they are called **typhoons**.

Tropical storms form over warm oceans, where the water temperature is more than 81 degrees Fahrenheit.

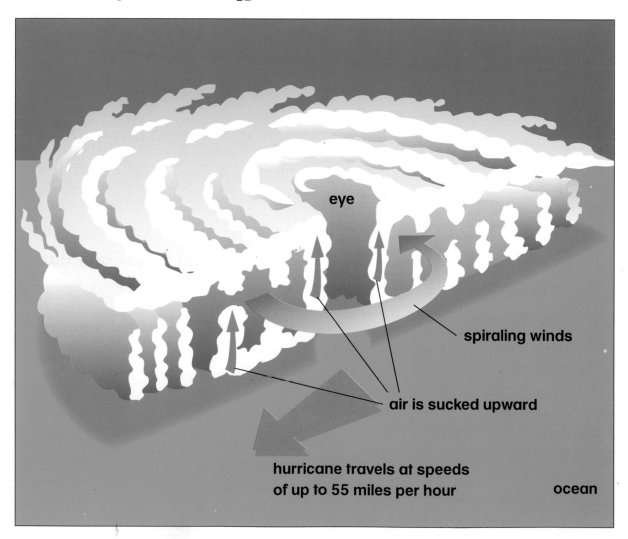

eye

spiraling winds

air is sucked upward

hurricane travels at speeds of up to 55 miles per hour

ocean

The mid-Atlantic Ocean, the Caribbean Sea, and the Gulf of Mexico have severe hurricanes. They usually happen in late summer or early autumn. This hurricane is dying down, but you can see the damage it has done along the coast.

Typhoons are common in the South China Sea and the Sea of Japan. They sink ships and damage harbors. Heavy rain from this typhoon has caused floods in Japan.

Each tropical storm is given a special name. This might make the storms seem friendly—but they're not!

Hurricanes are huge and violent weather systems. They bring high winds and dark clouds, which shed torrents of rain.

The center of a storm, called the **eye**, is calm. A belt of high winds, 100 to 150 miles wide, surrounds the eye. These winds **spiral** at about 110 miles per hour. Some winds can reach 185 miles per hour. The storm sucks in air at a low level and draws it upward into the atmosphere, to a height of about 6 miles.

TWISTERS!

Tornadoes are another kind of spinning storm. That is why they are sometimes called twisters. Tornadoes are usually between 500 and 5,000 feet wide at ground level—much smaller than hurricanes. But tornadoes are still very fierce. They arrive with a roar like an express train, often with flashes of lightning and crashing thunder.

Tornadoes are very common in Oklahoma, Kansas, Nebraska, and southern Iowa. This whole region is nicknamed Tornado Alley.

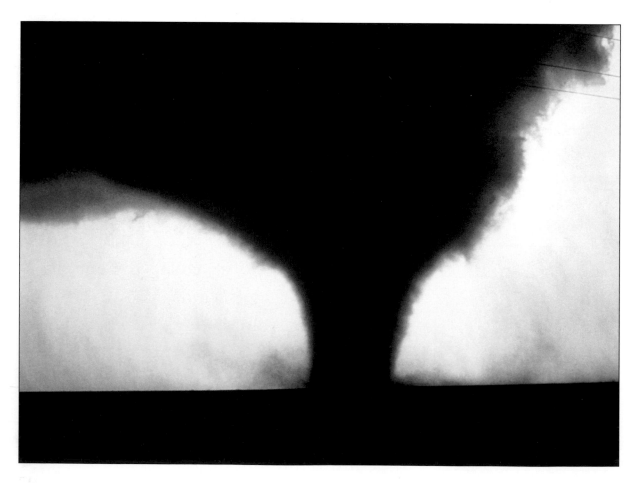

Over seas and lakes, a funnel cloud can whip water up into the air, creating a **waterspout**.

When a mass of cold air meets a mass of warm air, large **thunderstorms** may form. High winds at different levels inside a storm can create a spiral **air current**, which can spin at up to 300 miles per hour. The spinning air picks up dust from the ground, creating a dark **funnel cloud** in the sky.

The center of the funnel cloud has very low air pressure. Rising air currents lift roofs and rubble high into the sky. High winds can destroy whole buildings.

In the desert, hot, swirling winds can carry dust and sand into the air, creating a storm called a dust devil.

BLOWING IN THE WIND

Water vapor in the air turns into water or ice, which falls as rain or snow. Rain and snow fall because the tugging force of **gravity** pulls everything downward.

Rain and snow can fall gently, as **drizzle** or snowflakes, but storm-force winds will drive them down at an angle and at high speed. Heavy rain and snowstorms may bring flooding or deep **snowdrifts**.

A polar bear copes with one of the worst snowstorms, called a **blizzard**. Freezing winds fill the air with white snowflakes, making it difficult to see.

Monsoons are heavy seasonal winds that blow across the Indian Ocean. They pick up moisture from the sea and shed the water in massive rainstorms over southern Asia.

In deserts, winds whip up dust, which hangs in the air and darkens the sky. High winds cause dust storms, which blast everything with stinging sand and grit. The dust makes it hard to breathe and to see. High winds can carry sand for hundreds of miles, until it drops back to the earth with rainfall.

Storms blow heavy dust southward from the Sahara Desert in North Africa. The storms may pile up big heaps of sand called **dunes** and cover farmland in sand.

THU DER AND LIGHT I G

Electrical storms, or thunderstorms, happen when the lower layers of the atmosphere are warm and moist, while the upper layers are cool. The storms often happen on warm summer days.

These storms start inside **cumulus clouds**. Inside the clouds, the air shoots up and down. We call the rising and falling air **updrafts** and **downdrafts**.

Lightning that glows across a large area of sky and clouds is called sheet lightning.

Sometimes lightning streaks and zigzags across the sky. This is called forked lightning. The current is only about one-half inch across, but its glow forms a band several yards wide.

Here's what happens inside a thundercloud: Air currents move up and down, creating positive and negative charges. Lightning travels between positive and negative charges in the cloud and on the ground.

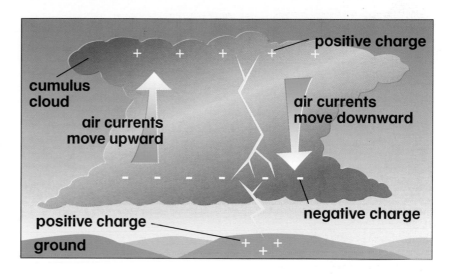

Lightning is made of **electrical currents**. They pass between positive and negative **charges** in clouds and on the ground. They travel at speeds of up to 87,000 miles per second. The current has a temperature of about 55,000 degrees Fahrenheit.

The great heat makes the air around the current swell, or expand. This action creates a **shock wave** that we hear as thunder. Light travels faster than sound, so we see the flash before we hear the bang.

See for Yourself

Watch a thunderstorm from your window, from the safety of your house.
- When you see lightning flash, start counting the seconds.
- Stop counting when you hear the thunder.
- Divide the number by five.
- The answer tells you how far you are from the storm (in miles).

HAILSTORMS

Hailstones form inside thunderclouds. They are made of water vapor that has turned to liquid and then frozen into small, hard balls of ice. Air currents toss the hailstones up and down at high speed, up to 100 feet per second.

As they move through the cloud, hailstones may melt and refreeze, growing larger each time. If you break open a hailstone, you can see several layers of ice.

In severe hailstorms, the hailstones sting your face and break the stems of plants when they hit the ground. They may lie frozen on the ground, forming an icy blanket.

Most hailstones are quite small. They measure about one-fifth of an inch through the middle. They look white because they contain tiny bubbles of air.

The longer the hailstones remain in the cloud, the bigger they get. One gigantic hailstone that fell in the Asian country of Bangladesh weighed more than 2 pounds!

When hailstones become too heavy to stay in the thundercloud, they fall. Gravity pulls them downward. Hailstorms usually cover only a small area of ground.

Hailstones are very hard. They hit the ground with great impact. If they hit a hard surface, they may bounce. These large hailstones have broken the windshield of this car.

FLASH FLOODS

Heavy rainstorms cause flooding if the water cannot soak into the ground. This happens when the soil has soaked up all the water it can. It is **saturated**. Flooding also occurs if the ground is very hard.

Flash floods are fierce, sudden, and unexpected. If streams and rivers cannot hold the rush of water, they burst their banks.

Bangladesh has more floods than any other country. The Ganges River overflows when it fills with melting snow from the Himalaya Mountains. Monsoon winds bring heavy rain. Cyclones from the Bay of Bengal attack the low-lying coast.

Gales and hurricanes at sea whip up huge waves. The waves drive against coasts and break over beaches, rocks, and harbors.

Rainwater swells the rivers, and they pour into the sea. As the river water meets the sea, waves pile up higher and higher.

When **tides** are very high and the weather is windy, great surges of water may travel up rivers and spill over low-lying land. Coastal cities may flood.

Rainstorms in desert regions are very rare. When they do happen, the water runs off over hard, baked ground, causing a flash flood. This flash flood is in the Sahara Desert in North Africa.

STORMS AND LAND

Storms erode, or wear away, soil and rock. Wind carries grit, which blasts the rocks, carving them into all kinds of shapes. Waves may rub against pebbles and boulders until the stones are round and smooth. Waves may eat away at cliffs, until the rock falls into the sea.

Soil may become saturated during heavy rains. If it is too heavy to stay in place, it may form a giant **mud slide**, which rolls down a valley. This mud slide is in Taiwan, Asia.

This pillar of rock is called the Old Man of Hoy. It is all that remains of a cliff in the Orkney Islands off Scotland. Storms have eroded the rock over hundreds of years. In the end, this pillar, too, will collapse into the sea.

Storms can also build up new land. Waves can deposit piles of pebbles, shells, mud, and sand along a coast. Over many years, these deposits may form long banks or beaches.

Electrical storms can attack the landscape, too. If lightning strikes desert sand, it can melt the sand, creating a kind of glass. Lightning sparks can set off forest fires. Fierce winds can fan and spread the fires across the country.

See for Yourself

- Some materials are harder to erode than others. Test them yourself.
- Collect various stones, pebbles, bits of clay, and pieces of chalk.
- Scratch them with a screwdriver. Can you cut any of them easily?

- Ask an adult to help you heat the items on a tray in the oven. Do any of them crack or crumble?

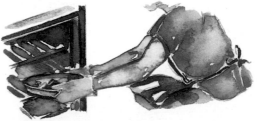

- Put the materials in a bowl of water and shake them around. Do they become soft or dissolve in the water?

NATURE FIGHTS BACK

It may take a long time for nature to recover from a severe storm. This woodland was destroyed by high winds in 1987, but it is growing again.

After a big storm or hurricane, the land can look as if it has been destroyed. Trees may have fallen to the ground like matchsticks.

But storms are natural happenings. In time, the trees will usually grow back again.

Some trees scatter their seeds in high winds. Coconut trees grow beside tropical beaches, and waves carry the coconuts from one island to another. New coconut trees will grow in the new places.

Animals and birds have adapted to stormy weather, too. The storm petrel feeds on small fish and squid. Powerful waves throw these creatures up to the surface of the ocean.

Many plants have **adapted** to stormy conditions so that they can survive. Tree roots spread out far and wide to anchor the trees against gale-force winds.

The giant sequoia tree grows in California. Its thick, spongy bark protects the trunk against lightning strikes and forest fires.

See for Yourself

- Collect seeds, nuts, and pinecones that have blown off trees.
- Which ones are designed to fly through the air?
- Which ones are designed to drop straight to the ground?
- Use a book to find out what kind of tree each one came from.

EL NIÑO

The pattern of weather recorded over a long period in a certain place is called its **climate**. Over thousands of years, climates have changed around the world.

In the past, people noticed that a warm **ocean current** sometimes flowed through the South Pacific. It brought stormy weather to South America around Christmastime. People there called it El Niño, which is Spanish for "the little boy," meaning the baby Jesus.

Waves crash over the rocks of the Galápagos Islands in the southeastern Pacific Ocean. El Niño has brought increased storms to the western coasts of the Americas and severe drought to Australia.

A severe hurricane in Honduras caused widespread flooding. It swept away houses and roads and ruined farmland. It may take more than 20 years to repair the damage.

In recent years, El Niño conditions have become more common. Scientists say that a warming of the earth's climate might be causing this change.

This **global warming** might be caused by exhaust fumes and factory smoke that have **polluted**, or poisoned, the atmosphere. These gases trap the sun's heat near the earth. Rising temperatures are making many parts of the world much stormier.

The Ganges River flows through Bangladesh. Near the sea, the river forms a maze of shallow waterways called a delta. Global warming could cause a rise in sea levels all over the world. If the sea level rose in Bangladesh, the delta and much of the country would disappear under the water.

MEASURING STORMS

Weather science is called **meteorology**. If the earth is becoming a stormier place, scientists will need to collect more facts about storms. That isn't always easy. A tornado or hurricane can wreck the instruments used to measure it.

Scientists measure wind speeds with **anemometers**. Some of these instruments have cups that catch the wind. As the wind rises, the cups whirl around faster and faster.

Out in space, **satellites** track the path of hurricanes. Satellites send back images of storms as they move across the oceans.

Some people have a barometer at home. When the air pressure changes, the needle swings around to tell us if good or bad weather is on the way.

Changes in air pressure tell us when a change in the weather is coming. We measure air pressure with an instrument called a **barometer**. We collect rainfall in rain gauges. A scale on the gauge shows how many inches of rain have fallen. Weather stations around the world collect facts about stormy weather to warn us of danger.

In Hong Kong, China, meteorologists give warnings about typhoons approaching the coast. People are told to move inland to safety.

GLOSSARY

adapted	Changed to survive in particular conditions
air current	A movement of air; wind
air pressure	The force with which air presses down on the earth's surface
anemometer	An instrument used to measure the wind's speed
atmosphere	The layer of gases around a planet
barometer	An instrument used to measure air pressure
Beaufort scale	A scale that describes the force of winds and their effects
blizzard	A severe snowstorm with high winds
brittle	Stiff and fragile; easy to break
charge	A buildup of electricity
climate	The typical weather in one place over a long period
condense	To turn from gas into liquid
cumulus cloud	A puffy, white cloud that sometimes brings thunderstorms
cyclone	A fierce tropical storm that takes place in the Indian Ocean
downdraft	A downward current of air
drizzle	A light, fine rain
dune	A high bank of sand piled up by the wind
elastic	Able to bend and stretch easily
electrical current	A stream of electricity that passes from one point to another
electrical storm	A storm that brings thunder and lightning
equator	An imaginary line that mapmakers draw around the middle of the earth
eye	A calm area at the center of a tropical storm
friction	The force that slows one object as it rubs against another
funnel cloud	A whirling, funnel-shaped cloud that drops from a thunderstorm, creating a tornado
gas	An airy substance that fills any space in which it is contained
global warming	The gradual heating up of our planet, possibly caused by air pollution
gravity	The force that pulls objects down toward the earth's surface
hurricane	A fierce tropical storm that takes place in the Atlantic Ocean, the Caribbean Sea, and the Gulf of Mexico

lightning	An electrical current that travels inside a cloud, between clouds, or between a cloud and the ground
liquid	A fluid substance, such as water
meteorology	The scientific study of weather conditions
monsoon	A seasonal rain-bearing wind in southern Asia
mud slide	A landslide created by water soaking into the soil
ocean current	A powerful stream of water passing through the ocean
poles	The most northerly and southerly points on a planet
pollute	To poison land, air, or water
pressure system	A huge mass of swirling air, with either high or low pressure
satellite	A spacecraft sent up to circle a planet. Satellites are used for research and communications.
saturated	Full of water and unable to soak up any more
shock wave	A wave of energy created by an explosion or intense heat
snowdrift	A bank of snow piled up by the wind
spiral	To spin around and around
streamlined	Slipping easily through air or water, with little resistance
thunder	A booming or crashing sound created when lightning heats up air very quickly
thunderstorm	A rainstorm accompanied by thunder and lightning
tide	A daily rising and falling of sea levels, caused by the pull of gravity from the moon and the sun
tropical	Relating to the tropics, the regions to the north and south of the equator
typhoon	A fierce tropical storm of the Pacific Ocean
updraft	A rising current of air
waterspout	A funnel cloud that forms or moves over the water
water vapor	The gas created when water evaporates
wind resistance	The force with which objects withstand the wind

INDEX